Earthy Talks

Asit Saha

Published by Asit Saha, 2024.

This is a work of fiction. Similarities to real people, places, or events are entirely coincidental.

EARTHY TALKS

First edition. December 12, 2024.

Copyright © 2024 Asit Saha.

ISBN: 979-8230359395

Written by Asit Saha.

Table of Contents

I dedicate this book to the misery, sufferings and ailments around the world.

Die! You will die someday.

Don't crave for it

Until the exit bell rings,

As long you are alive,

Leave an impact

For the others to hold the baton high

Chapters

Introduction

Introduction

Every person is born for fulfilling certain dreams. Sometimes, the external or internal hurdles deter the mission. The first step to heal is to gather umpteen motivations. Earthy Talks is a collection of motivational poems serving the purpose.

Chapter 1: Selfless Move

The world remains mum;
    When you want to;
    Raise a voice;
    For a cause
    The world remains blind;
    When you want to;
    Show your efforts;
    For eliminating a crisis
    The world remains dead;
    When you want to announce;
    You are alive.
    Keep moving;
    With selfless intent;
    Until, you save a distressed soul.
    May be, your reward awaits the next door.

Chapter 2: Platonic Relationship

Sitting under the tree,
I wanted to be free.
A fruit hanging from a branch,
Welcomed me from the heart
The reciprocation was instantaneous,
Our relation grew frivolous.
"How sweet I'm?" didn't reveal the fruit
But, the appeal was magnetic;
Compelling me to stretch my hands

Chapter 3: Just Act

Don't expect;
>Unless the miracle happens
>Perform your actions;
>To create some tractions!

Chapter 4: Arrogance – The Hidden Enemy

Palatial house,
    Sprawling lawns,
    Lavish dishes,
    Within-a-blink attentions
    All gone!
    Behind were the arrogant acts.
    The lost empire can be regained,
    If the efforts are empathized again!

Chapter 5: Life Exams

Sometimes, life conducts unexpected exams.
    Those, who dare,
    Score fare!
    The journey does not end here.
    More they get baked,
    Confident they become.
    With confidence enriching the experience,
    The seasoning becomes tastier.
    Rewards grow heftier.

Chapter 6: Teaching Technique of the God

Everyone knows,
Demons are evils;
Leading to destructions!
Why demons exist?
Humans always ponder.
Becoming helpless, they pray for an answer.
The god responds in silence;
By framing a plot!
He wants to teach a lesson on good over bad.

Chapter 7: Writing Through Eyes

When you start your day,
    That's the introduction.
    As the time tickles,
    And incidents occur,
    They become the chapters.
    Some may be worst,
    Some may be good,
    Ensure the conclusion;
    Remains sweet, lovable and enjoyable!
    Be positive, stay happy.

Chapter 8: The Delightful World

How delightful is the world?
Flowers dancing in breeze;
Populate the mind with fragrance.
How sweet is the world?
Bees sucking nectar from flowers;
Fills the heart with sweetness
How melodic is the world?
Birds flying and signing in harmony,
Entertain the mind with soft feels.
How courteous is the world?
Trees welcoming the tired travelers under their cool shades;
Offer respite for the next move.

Chapter 9: You're Resourceful

You are mindful;
> When you are helpful,
> You are powerful;
> When you are resourceful

Chapter 10: Always Reveal The Truth

Expressing remorse shoos people away.
Everyone loves living in a rosy wrap.
But, a few care for you.
You do not know who they are?
Always reveal the truth.
Those with you will stay.
They will surely show you the way;
Of overcoming a mishap
Keep moving.
You will meet;
Your well wishers;
When the time is right

Chapter 11: When To Stop?

When you act,
Someone will react.
If you react,
The situation deteriorates.
You will fail;
Reaching your goals;
You will lose;
The love bestowed from others.
Stop, when someone reacts!
Not getting attention;
Will make his intention silent
The way is clear, move again.

Chapter 12: Say 'Thank you'

Say 'Thank you' when you are awake.
Say 'Thank you' when you go for a deal.
Say 'Thank you' when you crack a deal.
Say 'Thank you' when you miss a deal.
Expressing gratitude;
Fills you with positivism
Positive feelings do not remind about the losses.
They motivate you to take a chance the next moment.

Chapter 13: You Can Always Help

If you can't lend;
 A small help,
 Then also you can help.
 Pray to the almighty;
 Because he is kind,
 If he doesn't listen today,
 He may respond tomorrow.

Chapter 14: Can't Discard The Requests

I was walking by a lane,
> The trees stood tall by a side.
> The lush green branches swayed in the breeze.
> They wished giving respite under their cool shade.
> Which tree to visit?
> I fell in a deep soup.
> An idea knocked my mind;
> Where I touched the trunks by changing the side

Chapter 15: Heartily reciprocate

If someone motivates,
Heartily reciprocate.
More is the exchange value,
Exponential rise is the face value.

Chapter 16: Genuine Grief

If your grief;
> Surpasses your tolerance and your weeps are genuine,
> A stone has to melt and flow as a stream;
> Where, you may quench your thirst.

Chapter 17: Government!

Government, government,
    We need a government;
    To win back rights;
    And stay at peace.

Chapter 18: Marriage – The Awaited Gift

Before the priest,
    With tightened wrist,
    Stands the groom;
    With happy eyes
    Before the priest,
    With smiling face,
    Stands the bride,
    Biting her lips
    They are in cloud 9,
    They are going to be;
    Each other's pride,
    They will be friends however.
    Their lives will glow forever.

Chapter 19: Adding Honey To Talks

A bit of honey;
    In talks;
    Begets friendly aura
    Diving deep;
    Into the others' sentiments;
    Foster painless settlement

Chapter 20: Real Stardom

Behind scene;
    Are the efforts put;
    For attaining stardom
    How many of us care?
    People not seen;
    On the celluloid are real stars.

Chapter 21: Eyes Speak Faster Than Mouth

If the mouth is shut;
    Under a threat,
    The eyes can speak faster;
    And pour wrath

Chapter 22: Shouldn't Be Weakened By Misery

I can't let:
Others die;
Because of my misery

Chapter 23: You Are The King Of Your Fate

Most of the decisions;
>Are made through shortcuts,
>Don't allow;
>Others to judge your fate
>It is obvious,
>Many of them;
>Fear your conscience.

Chapter 24: In Remembrance

She was the pendant;
    Of my life;
    Shining close to my heart
    May her soul;
    Rest in peace;
    In my heart again

Chapter 25: Big 'No'

There is always;
　A big 'no' from others;
　When you seek help
　They aren't equipped to;
　Feel the pain;
　You undergo at hard times.
　Time will be witness;
　When they;
　Become helpless

Chapter 26: Knowledge Is Light

Someone writes to emit light.
Someone reads to glow in light.
Knowledge is the light;
Keeping the egos out of the sight

Chapter 27: Act From Day One

As long there is ignorance,
    There is pain.
    As long there is fulfillment,
    There is gain.
    Be wise.
    You are the anchor.
    Act from day one.
    The world is yours.

Chapter 28: Dignity Is The Jewel Of Life

Dignity is the jewel of life.

People can remain alive;

Without food and water for some time,

Once the dignity is endangered, they are dead.

Chapter 29: The Wall Doesn't Matter

If your back sticks to the wall,
Do not drown yourself in grief.
You can still move on.
Abundant is the air,
Taking a deep breath;
Enhances your flair

Chapter 30: Sorry To Say

How ruthless are the people?
    Dividing the world with umpteen resources;
    With caste, creed and religion
    The same blood flows through the veins.
    The same pain is borne for growing foods.
    The same water quenches the thirst.
    Why the hatred rules?
    When the hearts beat together
    Really sorry! No words to explain.

Chapter 31: Propose

Let me ignite my sun;
    To spread some light
    Let me show my moon;
    To offer some respite
    I can make your life;
    Happy and industrious
    You may stay with me;
    Soulfully forever

Chapter 32: Importance of Hunger

The importance of hunger is felt;
When a baby cries for the mother's milk,
An orphaned child begs in front of a classy car,
Foods thrown into trash bins
The importance of hunger is also felt;
When the drought casts its spell,
Wars turning the granaries into rumbles,
People becoming jobless for no reason
Can we stop wasting foods?
Can we donate a penny for growing foods?
Can we distribute foods through camps?
Let not the hunger dampen the spirit of brotherhood!

Chapter 33: Don't Expect

Don't expect,
    Show respect.
    Eases the pain,
    Paving the path for gain

Chapter 34: Be Determined Like Sunrays

Whenever you feel low,
Think of the rising sun.
The sunrays penetrate;
Through the window panes;
Even if they are shut
Likewise, hurdles are the;
Closed window panes of life,
Your determination is the sunrays;
Guiding you to reach your goal

Chapter 35: Mourn When A Person Is Alive

Why mourn;
    After a person dies?
    Why not when;
    He was alive?
    He had basketful hopes;
    To be fulfilled;
    With your love and respect
    Why the flame of;
    Hatred and avoidance spread;
    Instead of rain filled with compassion?

Chapter 36: Stretch Out With Resources

If you think,
>   It's the end,
>   Let it be.
>   Stretch out,
>   Once the resources are replenished,
>   Material or immaterial

Chapter 37: Are We Compassionate?

The yells of the deprived
    Can't be unheard
    Because the god
    Resides among us
    The god teaches us
    To be compassionate
    Are we?
    We are the actionable gods equipped with resources.
    Staying close to the deprived
    Why we remain mum?
    Injustice ruling for long

Chapter 38: You Are The Sun

Why you get scared?
Do you know?
You lose the inner 'you'
When others come up with their views
You are the best
You ought to believe
You can spread the light
More than the sun
Instead of the fight,
Keep the egos out of the sight
You will feel light
And make the moment bright

Chapter 39: Nature of the God

If you are innocent,
> God is far from you.
> If you wish filling the gap,
> God may come closer to you.

Chapter 40: Live Like A Rock Star

Live like a rock star.
Your arrival must fetch applaud.
Your talks must resemble
The power chords of a guitar
Learn this art
If you want to
Become the apple of the eye

Chapter 41: Deploy Determination As Specs

When you walk the way,
    The fog may hinder,
    Making the vision blur!
    The determination;
    Is the specs
    Helping to overcome the hurdles

Chapter 42: Act Like Water

Flow like a river;
    If you wish irrigating hopes
    Fall like a spring;
    If you wish offering respite
    Water is precious,
    Abundant and multifarious
    Acting like the water,
    Makes the life blissful forever

Chapter 43: Celebrate To Explore The Truth

The sweetness of the truth
    Cannot be enjoyed in dreams
    There must a real-time celebration
    Where one should have the guts
    To speak the truth,
    And the other should be eager
    To listen the truth

Chapter 44: Weak Situation

The poison loses its strength;
    If it fails to kill the hatred,
    The love becomes a nomad
    If it fails to occupy the heart

Chapter 45: Who said I am poor?

Who said I am poor?
   My heart is rich in sorrows
   I experienced for years.
   My mind is prepared
   To take the flight for freedom;
   Like the birds flying to spot some grains.
   Who said I am poor?

Chapter 46: Poison Might Weep

The poison might weep
  If the deprived
  Decides for a suicide

Chapter 47: Your 'Inner You'

Realizing the truth
    Doesn't require a penny
    Or the external guidance from a monk,
    It can be felt from within
    Through deep thinking

Chapter 48: Don't Crave For Death

Die! You will die someday.
Don't crave for it
Until the exit bell rings,
As long you are alive,
Leave an impact
For the others to hold the baton high

Chapter 49: Feeling Vs Sharing

Whatever is felt; is the knowledge.
Whatever is shared; is the privilege.

Chapter 50: Earn Trust First

If you ignore,
>You cannot learn.
>If you haven't learnt,
>You cannot earn.
>Earning is not about the money.
>Money is the outcome of earning the trust.

Chapter 51: Putting Efforts For The Growth

The smell emitted from the torn soil;
After the first raindrops kissing it;
Is the sign for the respite and growth
Likewise, your new efforts;
Should motivate and obligate;
To sing the wind of change

Chapter 52: Hot As Cappuccino!

Your efforts
    Should be
    Hot as a
    Freshly brewed cappuccino

Chapter 53: Well Wishers Don't Pamper

Everyone around you
>Are not your well wishers
>Especially, those pampering you
>With rosy words
>Well wishers
>Don't speak much,
>They win your heart
>Through their guidance

Chapter 54: Isn't it?

You are alone
    When you seek help,
    You are flooded with people
    When you offer help

Chapter 55: Selfish Minds

Whom you thought were your own,
> They faded away after playing with your heart.
> They always loved their interests.
> They extracted as much they could from you,
> Gave lame excuses and moved to their next target

Chapter 56: Toxic Place

The place
    Where deploying fear is the practice
    For deriving fun,
    That place is not fit
    For a stay, work
    And growth

Chapter 57: The Giver Is The Sun

You are the sun
    When you offer help,
    The seekers are the planets
    Orbiting around you

Chapter 58: Serve Sans Losing The Nerves

How much you are exhausted;
    You only know.
    How much pain you bore;
    You only know.
    The dependents always depend on you;
    Not thinking of the time.
    You should be ready to serve
    By not losing your nerve

Chapter 59: Peace Within

The silence I
    Feel within
    Is the haven

Chapter 60: Window Is Our Mind

Window is our mind,
    When shut,
    The darkness
    Ruins from within
    When the mind
    Is open,
    Constructive thoughts flow
    Like fresh air

Chapter 61: Aim

The aim in life
   Should be
   Like a ship with sails
   Tearing the waves

Chapter 62: A Heart Can Win Hearts

If you want to
Win others' heart,
Ensure you have a heart

Chapter 63: Serve Like A Tree

Grow like a tree,
    Spread like its branches
    Under which the needy
    Can get respite

Chapter 64: The Innocent Suffers The Worst

The innocent suffers the worst
　　When vested interests clash
　　Who can protect the innocent?
　　The god is mum for decades.

ACKNOWLEDGEMENT

I am grateful to the pains and sufferings that have baked me hard to write these poems.

Asit Saha

13.12.24

Don't miss out!

Visit the website below and you can sign up to receive emails whenever Asit Saha publishes a new book. There's no charge and no obligation.

https://books2read.com/r/B-A-WRTEB-UZRKF

BOOKS 2 READ

Connecting independent readers to independent writers.

About the Author

Writes to motivate and entertain.